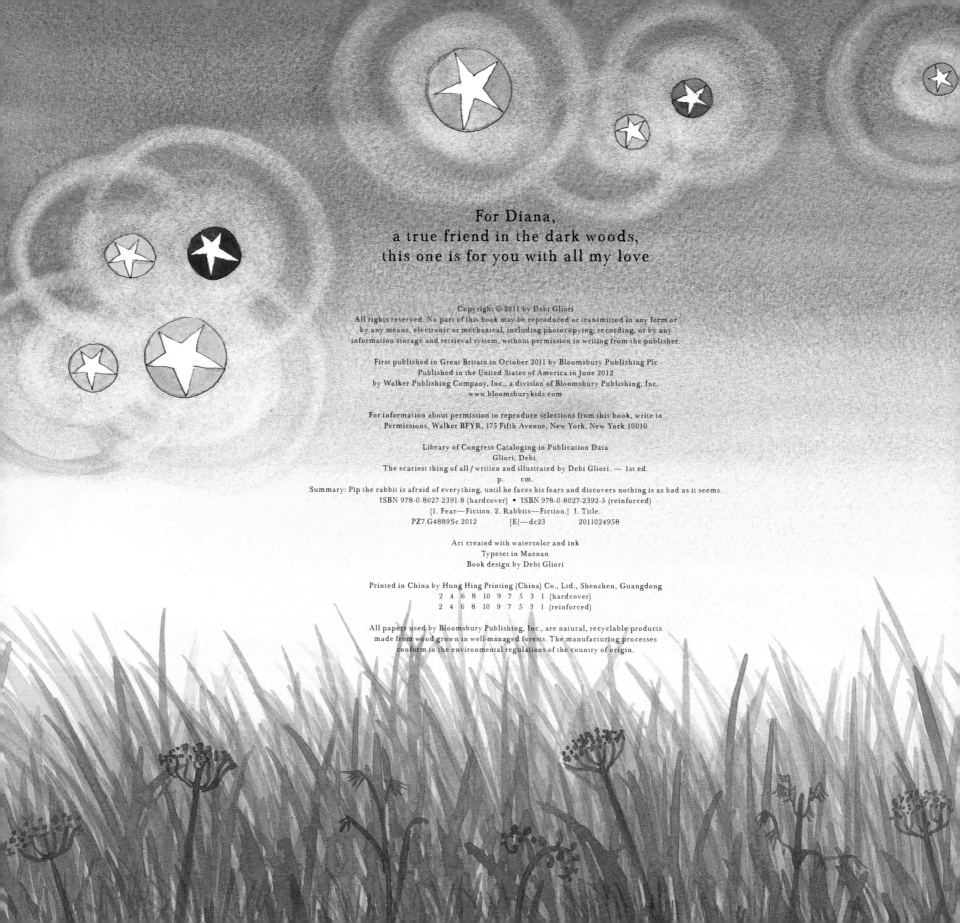

For Diana,
a true friend in the dark woods,
this one is for you with all my love

First published in Great Britain in October 2011 by Bloomsbury Publishing Plc
Published in the United States of America in June 2012
by Walker Publishing Company, Inc., a division of Bloomsbury Publishing, Inc.
www.bloomsburykids.com

For information about permission to reproduce selections from this book, write to
Permissions, Walker BFYR, 175 Fifth Avenue, New York, New York 10010

Library of Congress Cataloging-in-Publication Data
Gliori, Debi.
The scariest thing of all / written and illustrated by Debi Gliori. — 1st ed.
p.   cm.
Summary: Pip the rabbit is afraid of everything, until he faces his fears and discovers nothing is as bad as it seems.
ISBN 978-0-8027-2391-8 (hardcover) • ISBN 978-0-8027-2392-5 (reinforced)
[1. Fear—Fiction. 2. Rabbits—Fiction.] I. Title.
PZ7.G4889Sc 2012   [E]—dc23   2011024958

Art created with watercolor and ink
Typeset in Maenan
Book design by Debi Gliori

Printed in China by Hung Hing Printing (China) Co., Ltd., Shenzhen, Guangdong
2 4 6 8 10 9 7 5 3 1 (hardcover)
2 4 6 8 10 9 7 5 3 1 (reinforced)

All papers used by Bloomsbury Publishing, Inc., are natural, recyclable products
made from wood grown in well-managed forests. The manufacturing processes
conform to the environmental regulations of the country of origin.

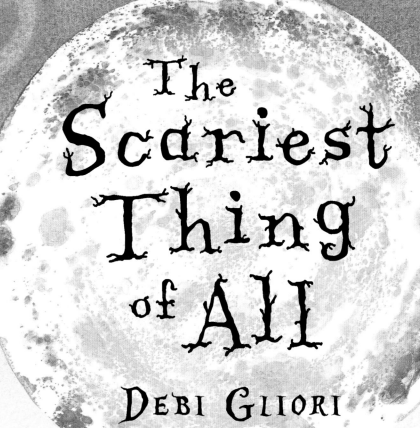

The Scariest Thing of All

Debi Gliori

Walker & Company · New York

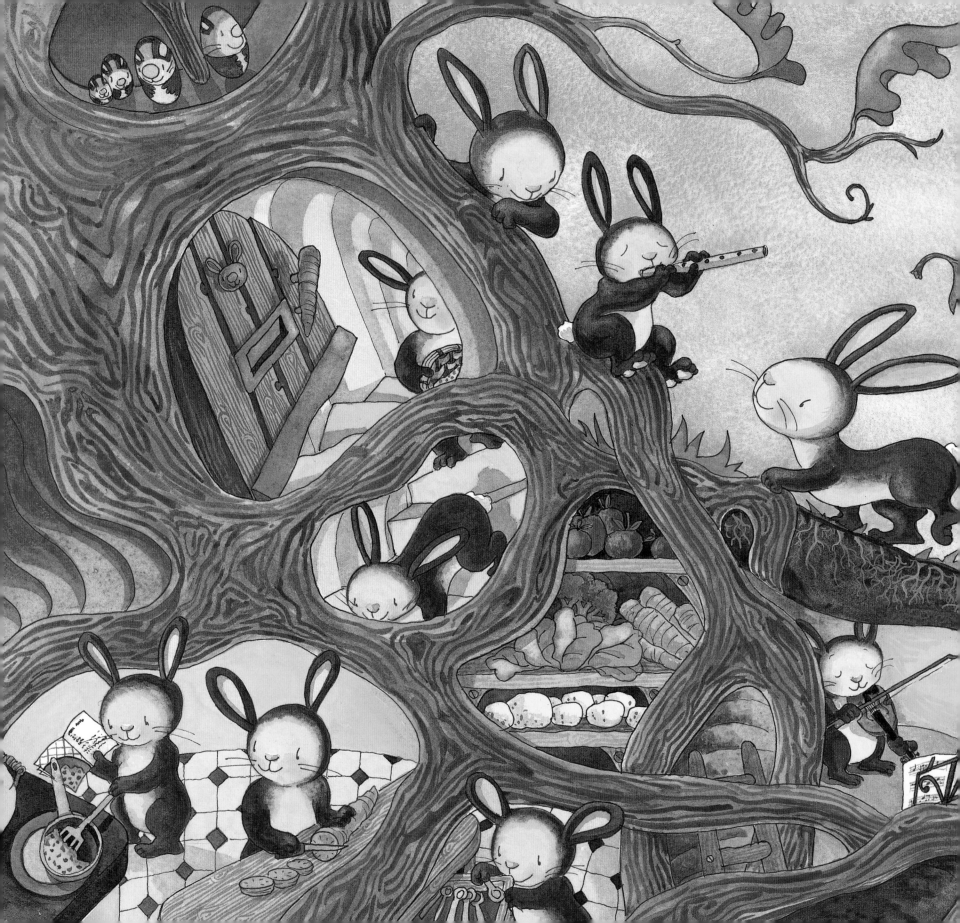

Once upon a wild wood,
deep down in a burrow, lived a family
of rabbits. There were big rabbits, medium-sized
rabbits, small-to-medium-sized rabbits, and one
very, very little rabbit named Pip.

Everything about Pip was small,
except the list of things he was scared of.

That was **enormous**.

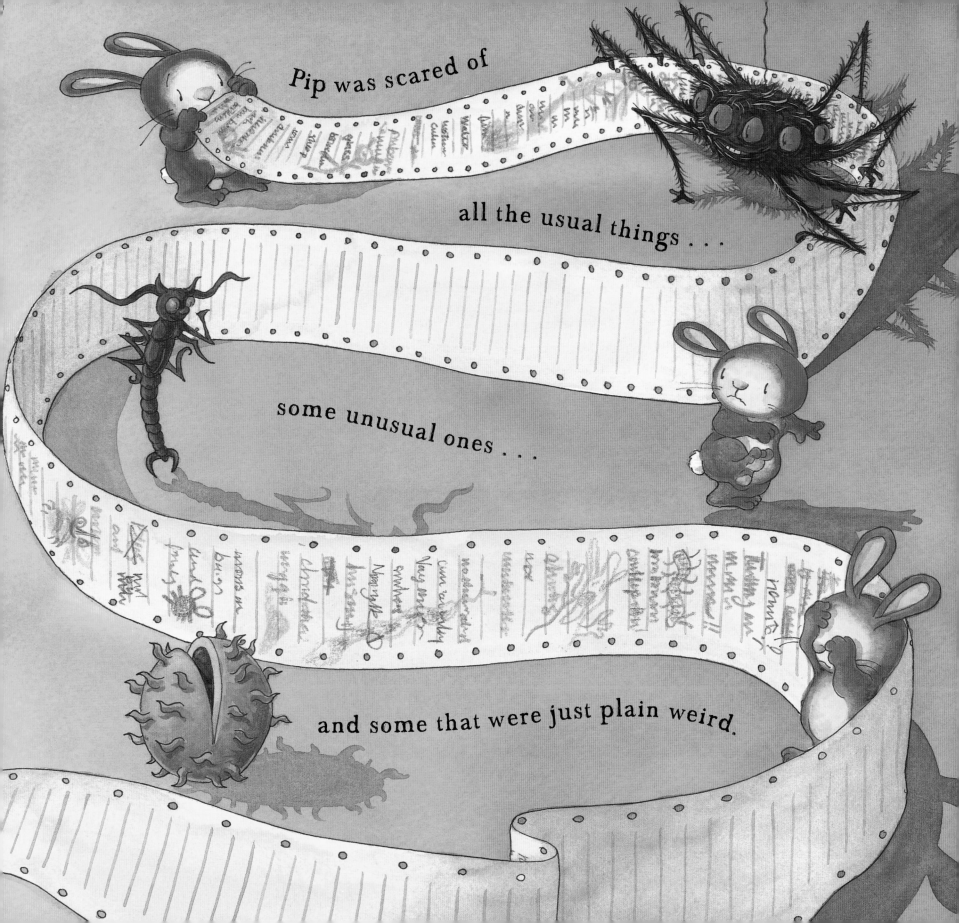

Pip was scared of

all the usual things . . .

some unusual ones . . .

and some that were just plain weird.

Poor Pip. He couldn't help it. To him, even the most harmless things were full of menace.

To Pip, the sound of rainfall was exactly like the sound a leggy wiggler makes as it weaves its web.

He just *knew* it was a gobbler blowing bubbles at the bottom of the lily pond.

Those tree stumps? Pip was 99.9 percent positive that they were the teeth of a giant wood troll.

And those fluffy pink clouds?
They looked just like—

STOP RIGHT THERE.

Poor Pip. Being scared all the time was very hard work.
One fretful day, after finding twelve new things
to add to his list, Pip pulled his ears over his eyes
and tried not to think.

Around him, his family worked in the garden.
Slowly, the day turned into afternoon.
The sun was warm, the grass was soft,
and very soon, Pip fell asleep.

When he woke up, it was dinnertime.

From across the garden came the smell of cooking.

Pip stood up to go home and that was when he heard it.

It came from right in front of him.

Raaaar, it went. Raar, raaaarrRRRR.

And then a little louder.

Raar. Raaar, rarrr, rarrrRRR.

Pip didn't stop to think.
(He didn't stop to add *Rarrr* to his list either.)
Pip turned and fled
into the dark woods . . .

. . . into brambles,

through haystacks,

across ditches, and under fences.

Pip fled as far from the RaaaaRRR as he could.

Then the moon peeked out from behind a cloud,
and Pip's eyes grew wide.
In front of him stood the biggest,
most enormous Scary Thing he'd ever seen.

Raaarrr, it said, raRRRR.

Pip took two steps
backward.

The Scary Thing
didn't move.

Rarr, it said.

R A R R R R R R R R R R R R R.

Pip trembled with fear
and clutched himself.

The Scary Thing
kept very still.

Rarrr,
went Pip's tummy.
RARRRRRRRRRRRRRRRRRRRR.

But the Scary Thing
kept quiet.

That's my tummy
making that noise,
thought Pip.
That means it's me.
I'M the Scariest Thing of All.
THAT's what I'm scared of. ME.

Pip took a big breath and said,
"I'm not scared of you,
Scary Thing.
I'm not scared of
Raaarrs
or rustling
or flapping
or hooWITing
or anything else on my list of
things to be scared of.
I'm not even scared of ME.

Pip waved good-bye
to the Scary Thing.

The Scary Thing
waved back.

On the way home,
Pip saw a gobbler
rise out of the lily pond.

"RRAAAAR,"

roared Pip. "I'm not
scared of YOU!"

In a flurry of bubbles,
the gobbler slid
back underwater.

The giant wood troll
thumped its stumpy teeth
at Pip as he passed.

"You don't scare ME!"
yelled Pip.

And the wood troll
had to agree.

When Pip was nearly home,
a leggy wiggler dropped out of the sky
and tried to drag him into its web.

Which was the last time
that leggy wiggler
was ever seen . . .

In the wild wood
they still tell tales of
the Scariest Thing of All.

Little gobblers
and wood trolls and leggy wigglers
pull the covers over their eyes
and hope the Scariest Thing of All
never comes back.

And
the Scariest
Thing of All?

It stood on its doorstep,
roared its loudest RaaAAAr...
and went inside
for dinner.